THE DYNASTY OF LAURENCE BURKE: LEGACY OF AN IRISH IMMIGRANT

By Bill Christy

Red Mountain Shadows Publishing
Cover Design by Serena Clarke
Printed in the United States of America on acid-free paper.

The Dynasty of Laurence Burke:
Legacy of an Irish Immigrant
By Bill Christy

ISBN-13: 978-1497558175
ISBN-10: 1497558174

Laurence Burke carved two large limestone posts and placed them at the entrance to his homestead. They guard the front of the home near the byway for all to see. Monuments to America, to the pioneer spirit, to the heart and soul of a young Irish lad who took the risk and followed a dream, Laurence Burke.

TABLE OF CONTENTS

Forward

In December 1933, an obituary was published in the Hutchinson, Kansas newspaper announcing the death of Laurence Burke. Laurence had died on December 18th, 1933 at age 84 years and 11 months. He died in his home on 6th Street, one block north of St. Teresa's Catholic Church. Laurence was survived by his wife, Kate, and three sons William, Edward and George. Laurence was to be buried in the Bean Cemetery, Little River, Kansas. George's wife, Mary Donnelly Burke, my grandmother, wrote Laurence's obituary and ended the obituary with a statement from her heart: "Laurence Burke leaves many virtuous and good works faithfully performed and the ones who have been privileged to live near him for so many years are indeed the richer for the experience."

There is ample documented evidence of Laurence's character and published events to write a Biography of his life. This book however is a Historic Novel with Laurence Burke telling his own story.

Introduction

Saint Patrick brought the four gospels of Christianity to Ireland. His conversion of the Irish was complete in the 5th century. The invasion of England in 1066 by the Norman Kings brought Catholicism to England and further to Ireland with the land grants to Norman English Lords. Lord William Burke received a grant in 1185, the Golden Valley in Central Ireland, Tipperary County. William built the largest Priory in Ireland, the Athassel Abbey along the River Suir. The invasion of Ireland by the Protestant King of England, William of Orange in 1660s transcended the Norman English grants and all the land reverted back to the King. He set out to remove all influences of the Papacy or other opposition to Protestantism from Ireland. Penal Codes were enforced against the Black (Catholic) Irish that disenfranchised them from Catholicism, land title, politics, education or professions. The King was determined to depopulate Ireland by starvation, deportation or other means.

Laurence's father, Henry Burke rented a five-acre farm along the River Suir that saved the family from the famines with other crops and livestock. Laurence having completed the allowed education for boys was employed to teach in the Loughmore Male National School. Following his conscience, he began teaching additional education to Black Irish children wanting secondary education. This was done in hiding and in direct violation of the Penal Codes. With the English closing in he was forced to immigrate to America in 1868. He made his mark in America. With hard work and honesty he found love, land and developed a family dynasty in Kansas, the heartland of America.

Born Into Famine

I was named Laurence (Larry) Burke, born to Henry and Anna Ryan Burke on January 19th, 1849. Mother was delivered in our family home with the village midwife assisting. We lived on a five-acre rented farm just north of the village of Loughmore, County Tipperary, Ireland. The small farm was located between the railroad track and the river Suir. We were a surviving family of six, Mother, Dad and my three older sisters Julia, Mary and Ellen. My sisters Anna and Bridget had died in infancy leaving over ten years between my next older sister, Ellen and myself. Being the only son and the heir apparent brought hope, pride and lineal property right into the home, but no relief from hunger. The potato crop lay rotting in the fields for the second year in a row. Ireland was in the worst year of famine it had yet seen.

My family, Black Irish (Catholics), survived the famine because of the land we farmed. Catholics could not own land under the penal codes enforced by the English law but rental rights made it possible for us to diversify with other crops, a cow, poultry and a few sheep on rented land. Tara (Land) was everything.

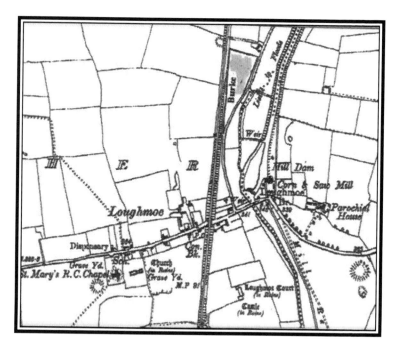

We could not survive without land. Rental rights were passed from father to son making me the heir apparent under the law.

I enjoyed the years spent working the farm alongside my father with my older sisters. I learned the trade of masonry from my father. We cleared the fields each year of field stones that turned up from working the land. We built stone fences and buildings from the limestone rock that littered the farm. Limestone meant good land but hard work. I became skilled at cutting and shaping stones. Masonry was a skill that followed me the rest of my life.

My family was very devout in spite of the Catholic religion being against the Penal Codes. Religious meetings such as Sunday Mass and any service by a priest were all violations of the Penal Code.

I attended the local grade school, the Irish National Boy's School, in Loughmore until grade eight and graduated with high marks. Catholic boys could not attend school beyond the eighth grade unless lessons were part of training for a trade. Girls could not progress beyond the sixth grade, as further education was deemed unnecessary for them by law. Higher Education violated the Penal Code along with political or professional careers.

Penal Code Text Book instructions to teachers: "PREFACE TO SECOND EDITION. Teachers should direct pupils to learn only such portions of the work as may be necessary for their intended occupations; for most pupils, the first and second sections and a few problems in the fourth and sixth will be quite sufficient". (Male National School Text)

Our faith and education went underground. We had services in homes and classes taught in hedge schools (out behind the hedge in hiding). I helped my family by teaching in the National School System and by teaching forbidden classes in hedge schools. The school system issued a single text for all the grades to each teacher who was instructed just how far to progress in the book each year. The only allowance was for boys in upper grades who were studying for a trade. The Penal Codes were enforced on all teachers of the Catholic children. As a teacher the book gave me the tool I needed to advance myself and to teach students beyond the allowed material. I felt good about helping my friends and neighbors but knew I was taking a risk if the English should find out. We were aliens in our own land.

South of Golden, Ireland on the banks of the River Suir stand the ruins of the Athassel Priory (Abbey), built in the year of our Lord 1192 by William Burke. William Burke formed Clanwilliamburke and ruled land granted to him by the English King John. His grant was "The Golden Valley" that included most of County Tipperary. William's sons formed other Burke Clans and the name became the most numerous name in Ireland. The Burke Clans were successful until the invasion of Ireland by the English Protestant King William of Orange in 1690 and the land reverted back to the English and Penal Codes were impressed.

Bill Christy

Black Irish

The Irish Catholics (Black Irish) were forced to submit to English Tyranny, be deported or emigrate out of Ireland. Demonstrations against English rule were taking place all over Ireland and the pressure was mounting. Men had little education, jobs, hope or future. The English Lords schemed to rid Ireland of all followers of the Papacy.

It all began with the invasion of Ireland by the Puritan Cromwell who destroyed many Catholic Churches and murdered the clerics. With the Invasion by the English King William of Orange the Penal Codes were enacted to outlaw any allegiance to the Pope. The Codes were designed to subject all of the Black Irish to complete dominance by the English King.

The population had grown to numbers that the land could no longer support. Every failure of the potato crop brought famine to the population. The backyard garden potatoes turned black with rot. The Landlords were converting land from potato crops to cereal grain, cash crops and exporting the grains for sale to England. They refused to provide any safety net for the population to survive on. The Landlords planned to depopulate Ireland one way or another and convert the land to large estates. The waysides and byways all over Ireland were jammed with starving vagrants trying to survive the English tyranny.

The Penal Code was applied to all Black Irish activities. Catholic Clerics were forbidden to hold services for Mass, funeral, baptismal, weddings or gatherings. Grave markers were not allowed. Education was restricted to primary schools. Land ownership, professional careers as statesmen, politicians, medical doctors or lawyers was strictly against the Penal Code. The English had ruled that the Black Irish were practicing mysticism in the way they danced with the rhythm of music and placed restrictions on body movement above the waist. The Black Irish responded by step dancing where only the legs and feet move. The Irish jig became popular. And even though the English language was required, the Black Irish continued speaking the Gaelic native tongue to prevent the English from understanding them. Nothing short of complete submission, deportation or emigration would satisfy the English.

Starvation, sickness and death covered the land like a cold wet blanket.

Bill Christy

The Isle of Tears

The plight of the Black Irish grew worse with every passing day. The Irish Republication Army (IRA) was active throughout the land. Pressure from the IRA to join forces against the English and the English enforcement of the Penal Codes along with the potato famine lead to millions of Irish dead, emigrated or deported. Ireland suffered the loss of over two million of its population in the late 1840's.

Most of the depopulation came from the youth. Starting a family in such an environment was not a choice. Young men could not hope to start a family. Young women found themselves looking into a life of servitude with a future of spinsterhood. The future was bleak.

My sisters Julia, Mary and Ellen, with their Letters of Reference in hand, went to the train station in Templemore where contractors were waiting and signed Contracts to become Indentured Servants to families in America. The Contractors were in it for the money and would not sign anyone they could not market in America.

Under the contract the girls were indentured to serve a period of three years in consideration for free passage, bed and board along with a small allowance working for an American household. The girls understood they would be chattel at the mercy of the Contractors but they had letters from other local girls who had indentured themselves with the contracts and were sold to American families who appreciated and respected them. They also learned that Sunday Mass was packed with young Irishmen looking for girls from home. The forever parting with the only family they had ever known and loved left a mark on all of us. We understood there was no turning back as they boarded the train for Queenstown and the ship to America.

In late 1867, there was a major uprising of Black

Irish youth in the towns of Templemore, Thurles, Cashel, and Tipperary. The English rounded up over 1000 youth, clad them in chains and transported them to the port of Queenstown to be deported to Australia. My family knew my days at home were numbered. The English were bound to discover my involvement in the Hedge Schools and my fate would be sealed. My sisters Julia, Mary and Ellen, having served out their contracts, had established themselves in America and were offering to help me with passage. The very thought of abandoning my aged parents and the consequences of their being without an Heir was too painful to speak about. Melancholy, Irish depression settled over the family.

May the Lord receive our spirit and let the devil take the hindmost.

Bill Christy

America is Calling

In January 1869, the English were closing in on Catholic youth in County Tipperary. Time was running out for me. My family knew my departure was imminent. Every knock on the door left us with dread. I must immigrate to America or be deported by the English to Australia. My uncle, Thomas Burke stepped up to take my place on the family farm. He is a blessing to us all. He was then and shall always be my Godfather and my hero.

My family and many friends traveled to the Templemore train station to see me off. My mother, father, Uncle Thomas and I knew this sad departure was forever. Mother's tears left a mark on me that never washed. We struggled to find words but settled for a final embrace and a few tearful glances. My way was made clear by my sisters who paid for the ticket. My travel was from Templemore by train to Elizabethtown, third class ship transport to New York City, USA and by train to Louisville, Kentucky. I was invited to live with my married sister, Ellen Burke Reitman and her husband, with a chance for work as a stone mason.

The Civil War in America had ended in 1865, the slaves were free and the Union of American States was secure. America had just suffered the greatest loss of young men in the history of war. The need for workers in mining, construction, railroads, steel mills and other industry had thrown the doors to immigrants wide open.

By departure time in Templemore, I had my ticket to Queenstown and my ship ticket to America in my pocket. Third class found me in a cabin with two sets of bunk beds, board and part time work in service to the ship. The journey took eighteen days and set me ashore at Fort Clinton, New York City where I was processed through US Customs.

At that time there was no Statue of Liberty or Ellis Island but simply the land of the free. The streets were not paved with gold but full of activity and people with places to go and things to do. I was full of excitement, wanting to find my place in it all.

At first I tried to avoid policemen but I soon learned they were all Irish with a ready handshake, a slap on the back and quick with the blarney. I felt like I had passed on and awoke in Heaven. I boarded the train to Louisville, Kentucky anxious to see my sister and to firm up the job I hoped was waiting for me.

Bill Christy

An Irish Stonemason in Kentucky

The Reitmans met my train in Louisville and welcomed me with open arms. They took me to their home on South Brook Street. It was a large two-story home, similar to other houses on the block. Ellen had made her mark. Her home was tidy and well appointed, as was the room rented to me. I always felt welcome, safe and warm in the Reitman's home. I soon got over the dread every time I heard a knock on the door.

Louisville was a bustling city full of people of all races and religions. Our neighborhood had many Irish immigrants. Catholic Churches were open all over town. I joined with the Reitmans and attended St. John's Cathedral about six blocks east of their home. I was amazed at the size and structure of it with the red brick exterior going all the way up to the bell towers. The inside was a work of art with stained glass windows, marble statues and seated 750 people.

Laurence's favorite Apostle was John, the most beloved. The story of John, who at the age of 19, stood at the foot of the cross of crucifixion looked up into the face of our Lord Jesus, their eyes met and Jesus spoke "behold your mother". John instantly understood he was charged with being a dutiful son to the Blessed Mother Mary and Jesus knew John would never fail her. John at his young age with the women did not present a threat to the Jewish hierarchy or the Romans.

Ellen introduced me to most of the people she knew and they all wanted the latest news from Ireland. She introduced me to Michael and Ellen Fahey, the family who lived next door. Mr. and Mrs. Fahey had emigrated from Ireland to Ohio. They moved to Louisville after their daughter Catherine (Kate) was born. Kate had grown into a lovely young woman who was never at loss for words. There was something about the glint in her eye and the spring in her step that caught my eye.

I reported to my new job at the stone quarry for a tryout and was hired. I was familiar with the stone we worked but the tools were new to me. The hard steel tools they used made the work faster, better and easier. We had lots of work to do as business was brisk and everyone was in a hurry.

Louisville was a city of monuments.

Bill Christy

The Girl Next Door

The Faheys invited the Reitmans and me to their home for Sunday dinner after Mass at St. Johns. The Faheys were very kind to me and I thoroughly enjoyed conversing in the Gaelic tongue with them. Kate was not fluent in Gaelic but her brogue was pretty thick and she constantly practiced her English.

After the blessing, Kate insisted on demonstrating the proper use of the finger bowl to me. I knew she was teasing me. I could not deny or explain the joy I felt. From the smiles on the face of those seated at that table it was obvious she was sparking a flame that might well be eternal. I was older and taller than Kate but I knew she would never be less than my equal.

Kate and I took our time but grew in understanding each day. It is no wonder I could not imagine a future for me without her in it. My love for her was certain but putting our lives together would be another matter. What is a man without land? I could never start a family without my own land to provide for them.

Kate, who is never at a loss for words, was speechless when I proposed marriage, offering her a ring and my solemn promise. She nodded her acceptance through her tears.

Love and land are the only things that last.

Go West Young Man

The railroads were advertising FREE LAND IN KANSAS. Kansas was being prepared for settlement. Land grants were being offered with the only consideration being that the claim holder was obligated to live on and improve the property as well as plant trees within a five-year period. They were called "Tree Claims". The amount of land in each claim was 160 acres of land, suitable for dry land farming.

I finally convinced Kate this was the only way we could have a future together. I had saved some money to buy the special ticket the Railroad was offering and boarded the train in Louisville. The trip would continue to the end of the railway and into the Wild West to free land in Kansas.

The Indian wars were still being fought. General Sheridan was given command over the 7th Army with many army camps placed in central Kansas to protect the settlers. General Sheridan had chosen Bill Cody as the head scout for his army. General Custer was commanding the unmerciful resettlement of the Warlike Plains Indians. Some small Indian tribes were overlooked, camped on the minor rivers and flood plains. The Army could not be everywhere; the Santa Fe Trail was being protected by small Army Camps. The trailhead was constantly moving west with the coming of the Railroad.

After three days travel, I departed the train in Salina, Kansas, the end of the finished train track. With my knap sack and a suitcase I started walking south toward the Santa Fe Trail looking for unclaimed land suitable for farming. My savings were about gone and time was running out to find a suitable claim.

I followed the Santa Fe Trail and joined a wagon train of merchants headed for Santa Fe. To my surprise, the friendliness and cooperation between us was a spirit of good will that will never be forgotten. The fact that I was without funds never came up. I could earn my board by simply working my way helping others.

I was constantly scouting the land around us as we traveled. We found the big cottonwood tree marking the Little Arkansas River crossing. The wagon master paid the fifty-cent fee per wagon and we made the crossing before making camp. The crossing was located about fifty feet south of a rock dam on the river and was layered with rock to make passage possible. The crossing had very steep banks about fifteen feet high with the river being ten feet wide. Most of the wagons needed an extra team to make the grade. The wagon master paid a fee for all of the wagons and livestock to be secured inside the Stone Corral overnight. Camp Grierson was nearby on the Little Arkansas River bank with a detachment of Black Soldiers of the 10th Army Division assigned to the 7th Army under General Sheridan. A Trading Post stocking supplies for the travelers was also nearby.

Soldiers were posted along the Santa Fe Trail

to protect the travelers from Indians and Outlaw Gangs. Most of the eastern Indian Tribes had been compressed into Kansas during the early eighteen hundreds. After the Civil War, General Custer, under the Command of General Sheridan, had been ordered to move all of the plains Indians into reservations in Oklahoma or far to the north. In some cases the removal was without mercy and resulted in many battles. Locally the Kansa Indians were enemies of the Pawnees. The Kansa Indians had been successful in pushing the Pawnees into Nebraska in the early eighteen hundreds. But with most of the Kansa Tribe moved to the Oklahoma Reservation, the Pawnees still had buffalo hunting parties coming through the area. Pawnee hunters could turn into warriors if the opportunity came. Outlaw gangs from the breakup of Quantrill's Raiders of the Civil War left many gangs as rebels without a cause that were a threat to Merchant wagon trains heading either way on the trail. The James, Younger and other gangs knew the merchants heading to Independence, Missouri had cash or gold to buy merchandise.

In the early morning, I watched the Merchant Wagon Train depart, heading up the hill westward.

Some of the merchants and I became friends and I knew they would be coming back someday. I decided to stay in the area for a few days and scout for unclaimed land suitable for farming.

I spent a few evenings around the campfire with the detachment of Black Soldiers of Camp Grierson. They had been slaves freed by Lincoln who had joined the Yankee Army and wound up fighting Indians. We exchanged stories about their slavery and my Black Irish background. They were honorable and brave men. They had lost eleven of their comrades, six in battle and the rest to illness. I felt safer knowing they were in the area ready to defend the settlers. We exchanged respect and friendship.

Later while scouting south along the Little Arkansas River, I met a small group of Indians. They invited me to their camp where we shared rations. Red Star, the Chief, spoke broken English and along with sign language we managed to communicate. He was the leader of five families of Kansa Indians who lived by hunting and gathering food along the river bottom. Most of their tribe had been moved to the reservation but his small group had been left alone.

Red Star noticed that I was interested in the way the women dried meat and fruit. They also stored grass seed in woven baskets for later use. He explained to me that to the south were sand hills abundant with game and fruit that sustained them with plenty to eat. We agreed to trade if I filed a land claim in the area. He advised me to look several miles west to high ground to avoid the flooding problems of the river bottom. We parted friends and I knew I had nothing to fear from the local Indians.

I found myself in awe of the Stone Coral. It had a wall about eight feet high and thirty inches thick and was about 300 by 200 feet in area. The rock was laid dry without mortar. Windows in the rock were spaced about fifty feet apart with a ten-foot gate opening to the river. William D. Wheeler had built it in 1865 and disappeared shortly thereafter. Nathan Bean was the current owner of the Stone Corral, the River Crossing, the Trading Post and Post Office. The Stone Corral was an amazing structure in the wilderness. I found the source of the rock, a large quarry with an endless supply of limestone rock. I knew I had found work if I decided to stay.

The Stone Corral and Little Arkansas River Bridge were built before the Civil War. The Bridge was burned down by the Indians. Nathan Bean replaced the bridge with a rock-lined ford. The Corral had been defended in 1865 by Buffalo Bill Mathewson, Captain Charles Christy and two other men with a six pound cannon and carbine rifles.

With the sun still high in the east, I walked up the trail about five miles to high flat ground and located an unclaimed piece of land with several springs, just off of the Santa Fe Trail. I located the claim marker and raised it on high with my thanks to the Lord Almighty.

Early the next morning I borrowed a horse and headed straight for Larned, Kansas to record my homestead claim. I had enough money sewn into my coat to pay the recording fee. In the year of our Lord 1872, this Irishman became a homesteader in Kansas. I mailed a letter from Larned to Kate, putting her on notice that a shelter for two would soon be under construction.

My land: where the deer and the antelope play.

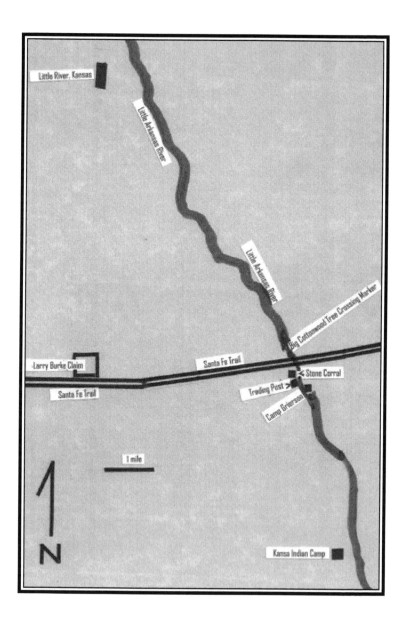

The Pioneer Spirit

The west was wilderness without law, schools, churches or doctors. The only help available was what we gave to each other. A man's word was his bond. Character and labor were all we had to live by and it worked. A Pioneer Spirit existed between the settlers, travels and merchants that transcended all the differences between us. Construction of homes, churches, schools, barns, putting in crops and harvesting them were community projects.

God had fed the followers of Moses by providing manna from heaven. God provided for me with overloaded wagon trains on the Santa Fe Trail. Provisions were constantly available from abandoned livestock, furniture, barrels, wagon parts, harness and tools. Many of the settlers were trying to transport their eastern homes to the west and the wagons could not withstand the loads put on them. It gave me a start on the lone prairie and I came to appreciate my location next to the Santa Fe Trail.

I learned the first night of bedding down on the prairie that the rattlesnakes enjoyed my warm blankets as much as I did. The only fuel for a fire was buffalo dung. It reminded me of the peat we burned in Ireland. It had its own perfume that filled the air and spoiled the aroma of the coffee. I found a wagon box on the trail and put a foundation of rocks under it that was rattlesnake proof. It was a new world at night looking up into the moon and stars, listening to the coyotes howl and yelp, the hoot owls call, the night bird's song and the constant buzz of rattlesnakes.

I mentioned the rattlesnake infestation to Red Star. He showed up at my camp the next morning with four Indian families and proceeded to hunt, capture, skin and butcher rattlesnakes. They knew what rocks and limestone outcroppings to look under. Not only was rattlesnake a favorite food of the Indians, they also used every piece of it, including the rattle. They gathered hundreds of rattlesnakes and pretty well solved my problem. The Indians left me a basket full of fresh fruit from the sand hills. It pays to have friends on the wild prairie. This was a good deed I shall not forget.

Most of my early days were spent gathering wagon parts, farm tools, kitchen utensils, barrels and other cast offs discarded by overloaded wagons on the trail. It did not take long before Nathan Bean, who owned the Trading Post next door to the Stone Corral Post Office, and I were constantly trading goods and tall stories. I did not charge him for the Irish malarkey even though he enjoyed it. I told him it was my job to recycle the goods he sold to people they could not haul up the Kansas hills. In the bargain I was able to put together a buckboard wagon and a team of horses and other supplies I dearly needed.

Nathan Bean owned and operated the Little Arkansas River crossing and the Stone Corral. I told Nathan about my experience and interest in stone masonry. We struck a deal to partner on stone I cut. He wanted help with the constant repair of the river crossing due to flooding. I ordered some cutting tools from Louisville, Kentucky and was soon in business. I was able to build stone skids as well as wagons to move and transport stone from wagon parts I scrounged up on the Santa Fe Trail. I soon had more going on than I could handle and bartered for help from local settlers and a few Indians.

I was surprised by the amount of cash and gold I received in payment. The settlers and Indians had no money but everything I did for the Army was paid in coin by the paymaster and most of the business I did with merchant wagon trains was paid for in gold. Nathan and I usually used cash or bartered goods as a settlement between us. I kept my word and made good on any deal that turned sour.

Nathan told to me that he was overwhelmed with the amount of trade goods I was bringing to the Trading Post and he could not continue buying. We agreed to a new bargain where the Trading Post would accept everything I brought in on consignment. We would split the proceeds of each sale half and half. My half would be applied to an open book account with the store. All sales to me or to any of my associates on anything other than the merchandise I supplied would be priced at twice the Trading Post's cost and charged to my open account. This gave him the financing he needed to continue and gave me bargain prices on his regular merchandise. It also provided a way for me to pay my workers in merchandise. We were financing each other and it was very profitable to both of us.

The time I spent with the soldiers at Camp Grierson made it clear the black troops were on terrible rations. Salt pork and hard tack was not enough for any man. I gave a wagon to the Indians and made a deal with them to deliver fresh fruit, game, buffalo and dried meat to the soldiers. I then talked to the Quartermaster about paying for the delivered food at bargain prices within his budget. I had to wait for payment but the Army paid in cash. I paid the Indians by taking them to the Trading Post and charging what they needed to my open account. The Indian women were very happy with the cast iron kitchenware, cook stoves, storage containers, and blankets. Everyone liked the deal because all of us came out on top.

The deal with Nathan Bean made my business possible. It financed my operations by paying my workers with supplies they needed. Many of the homesteaders settled without a dime to their name but were willing to work for supplies or equipment I could provide and it increased Nathan's business and profits several times over. I needed men to work as teamsters, quarrymen, cattlemen and farm hands.

Most of all, it gave me the capital to plan for a new life with Kate and a new house.

I began excavating a dugout to construct a sod house on the homestead. While my farmhand and I watched a few wagons come up the trail, the last wagon broke an axel. As the driver jumped from the wagon, his heel caught and he flipped out headfirst. We hurried to his aid but nothing could be done. His head had landed on a rock and he died on the spot.

The wagon was overloaded beyond its capacity. His family was in the wagon but unharmed. His wife and four young daughters felt like the world had ended for them. She explained that this move to the California gold fields had been her husband's idea and she refused to move one step more to the west.

After a long discussion we struck a bargain. In exchange for her wagon and four mules, I agreed to furnish a coffin, bury her husband on a hilltop overlooking the Santa Fe Trail, cut and place a rock slate over the grave and place a marker on it. I also agreed to transport her and her family to a railhead and buy tickets for them along with paying the freight bill to ship whatever she wanted out of the wagon and pay her cash for the difference in value for the wagon, mules, and whatever she left in the wagon.

I estimated she could be back with her family in St. Louis within ten days. Marie La Font and I shook hands on the deal.

I gave my farmhand instructions on moving the broken wagon and the four mules to my homestead. I wrapped her husband's body in canvas and loaded it on my buckboard along with her, the children and their luggage. I drove back down the Santa Fe Trail to the Trading Post where I knew they would be accommodated. She picked out a wooden casket that went on my account along with their room and board expense.

Early the next morning, I returned to the Trading Post. I loaded the casket and the family to return to the burial site near my homestead. My farmhand and I had already dug the grave. After the graveside service we drove the buckboard to my homestead to transfer what she wanted shipped to St. Louis from her wagon to mine. We stopped by the Trading Post where Nathan gave me access to my strongbox in his safe. I removed gold and silver coins and paid the lady per our agreement. The relief on her face made the trade worthwhile. The next day we headed for McPherson, the closest railhead, as promised.

I had several reasons to feel good about our bargain. I now owned four of the finest mules ever produced in Missouri and a new Conestoga wagon that was to become my temporary home while the soddie was being constructed. The rest of the load sweetened the deal. Tools, farm implements, two Colt pistols, two Winchester repeating rifles, one long barreled Henry repeating buffalo rifle along with cartridges, shells and plenty of black powder. There was also a wood stove, furniture and more than enough kitchen equipment to get Kate and I started in the soddie.

Home on the Range

I stationed several water barrels at the edge of my homestead next to the Santa Fe Trail with a sign on the barrel, "Free drinking water for the asking." A cool drink of fresh sweet spring water was there for everyone, including their animals. The drink was free but we bartered on any water to be hauled off the property. Free for the drinking not for the taking. Business was brisk and profitable. The world passed before my door.

I will always remember a very tall lanky good looking, well met, gentleman with long wavy hair who stopped by for fresh water. He was wearing a deerskin jacket and riding on a fine buckskin horse leading six pack mules. Buffalo Bill Cody showed me the Medal of Honor that the US Congress had awarded for his bravery while serving under General Sheridan. Bill was chief scout for Sheridan when the Army caught up with Yellow Hand and his tribe running away from the reservation. Yellow Hand recognized Bill Cody and offered to settle the issue by a fight to the death between them. Without consulting General Sheridan, Bill accepted the challenge. The Indian Tribe and the Army stood by as Yellow Hand and Bill Cody went toe to toe.

When the dust settled, Yellow Hand was dead and Bill Cody was still standing. The issue was resolved and the Indians returned to the reservation. Bill was never without words but his deeds preceded him. Bill was the first Kansan to receive the Medal of Honor.

Bill's family lived in Lawrence, Kansas. He was headed west to work for the railroad as a contractor to supply buffalo meat to the railroad workers. Bill Cody had a better understanding and respect for the Plains Indians than anyone I had ever met. I gifted him all the water he wanted, no bartering necessary.

Merchant wagon trains always brightened

my day. I became acquainted with many of them as friends and business partners. Jon De Baca and Roberto Martinez were two such acquaintances. I could order horses, mules and farm equipment from them on their way to Kansas City and the Missouri River trading centers and they would bring them to me on the return trip. Merchants could buy goods in Kansas City for one tenth of what the same items would cost in Mexico City.

We talked about the coming of the railroads and what the future would hold for our business. They assured me they would be coming my way until the railroad reached Santa Fe. Wagon trains were just too vulnerable to outlaw gangs and Indians. They told me about their merchant relatives, the Chavez family, who had been murdered and robbed by a rebel gang just a few miles west of my homestead. But this had happened before the Army had opened Camp Grierson. A new day was coming for my trading operations.

With the coming of the railroads and the end of the Santa Fe Trail traffic, Nathan Bean and I had many discussions about the future of our business arrangements. We had five to ten years left at the most. We traveled to Kansas City to get a glimpse of the future. Kansas City had become a wholesale supply center for the west with a good deal of its products being manufactured there. Kansas City was preparing to become a major market for the west. Huge flour mills and grain storage bins were under construction along with large stockyards for trading cattle and hogs. Packinghouses to slaughter and market meat were going strong. It was clear to us that the railroads presented a clear path for farmers to sell their products for cash. That trip was an eye opener for me. I knew we needed to keep up with what was going on in Kansas City. It was defining our future. And it was clear that our future would turn to livestock and farming.

The railroads were bringing the east to the west. Hutchinson, Kansas was becoming a crossroads for four national railroads. It would soon be a major trading center for farmers and farm products. Farmers needed a way to get to market and did not have the roads to do it. Access to railroads was a must for any community to thrive.

I ordered a horse drawn road grader to be delivered to McPherson, Kansas. I intended to make a beginning and I had the mules and horses to help. If the homesteaders were to survive, we needed passable roads to the markets.

Midmorning on September 18th, 1874, a dark cloud formed in the west that grew and became more ominous the closer it came. A strange noise preceded it unlike anything we had ever experienced. The day went from sunlight to dark as the black cloud descended on us. Vast swarms of grasshoppers covered everything in sight. The grasshoppers devoured the grass, weeds, melons, trees, corn, cornstalks and the clothes that were hung out to dry. The sound was deafening and unnerving. They covered the land two to four inches deep and caused panic. After everything was gone they moved on to the east.

The only thing left for us to survive on was the food and grain that was protected by containers or bins. Some of the farmers saw this as a Biblical sign to drive us out of Kansas. Others just wanted out. They all agreed that California was the place to go. I did everything I could to convince them to give their farms another chance. I offered sharecrop agreements to anyone who wanted to stop farming or who could not afford to farm the next year. In addition, for those farmers who would not stay, I signed an option to buy them out after they perfected their land patents. This way, they could at least save their investment in the land. I would do the planting and harvesting and pay each farmer one third of the harvest.

Most of the farmers who stayed needed help. I agreed to work all or part of their farms on the shares if they would hang on. We needed each other to survive the worst grasshopper plague Kansas ever had.

Nathan invited me to the warehouse to introduce a new product that had just come in: barbed wire. No more staking out horses at night or herding cattle. We could fence in our homesteads and turn the livestock loose. We had corrals but the livestock had to be out on the prairie to feed on the grass or crops. Nathan and I knew the wire would work well with stone posts. We agreed I should increase our production of cut stone posts. It suddenly made sense for the government land development planning to have every section of land with public easements on every side of the section lines. The open range would soon become history in central Kansas.

On November 23rd, 1874 I applied for U.S. Citizenship in Rice County, Kansas. It would take me five years under the law to become a citizen, but it was well worth the wait. I was proud of it and I never looked back.

I did not have success in raising spring wheat. It would not mature ahead of the summer drought. A large settlement of 1500 Mennonites, immigrants from Russia, had settled east and south of our township and introduced drought-resistant Turkey Red Winter Wheat. A Godsend to Kansas farmers.

In 1875, the Census taker found me in my Bachelor Hall, proud of the completed soddie. I had lined the dugout with fieldstone and used plowed-up sod above the ground level. The sod looked rough but it insulated the living space and kept it livable. I had cut stone from the quarry to make steps up to ground level and framed in a roof. I knew Kate would probably faint at first sight. She had drawn up plans for a new house we were going to build that was very similar to her family home. But I wanted to start construction after she arrived. The winters were too cold for the Conestoga wagon so we would start our lives together in the soddie. We were making plans for a grand wedding at St. Johns in Louisville, Kentucky in 1877.

A patrol of Buffalo Soldiers dropped by my

place one day. We had lunch and they refreshed themselves with spring water. I learned General Custer was killed in the Indian War on the banks of the Little Big Horn River. Custer's horse Comanche was the only survivor. I knew this was the last stand for the plains Indians. The army would never let up till they were all on reservations. The soldiers indicated this should not be a problem for our friends, the Kansa Indian camp. Sergeant Johnson told me he had seen signs of Pawnee Indians about two miles west of me on the Santa Fe Trail.

Kate would arrive next year and I hoped the Plains Indian problem would be resolved before that. The soldiers made a point of stopping by my place at every opportunity. They were looking after me and I appreciated it.

A Deal In Wheat

The grasshopper plague of 1874 left few hearty souls remaining to start over again and get new crops in the ground. I hauled in many wagon loads of Turkey Red Winter Wheat seed, bought from the Mennonites. I rounded up all the men I could and we started planting in the fall of 1875. I had the resources to do it and I was in with everything I had. We planted my claim, the claims I had sharecropping agreements on, and everyone else who would pay or barter. The farmers with teams of horses or mules and every team I owned were put to work in the process. We planted every acre that was sod broken and under tillage. The wheat grew well in early fall but went dormant and lifeless with the first freeze and the coming of winter. The winter was hard with heavy deep snow.

Spring came early in 1876. The green wheat, to our relief, came alive. The spring rains came softly and timely. In late May the weather turned hot and dry. I met with the local farmers and proposed a plan to market our crops. We came up with a rough estimate of how many bushels of wheat we could produce. I traveled to McPherson, Kansas for a meeting with the railroad people and made a deal for twelve boxcars to be stationed at the closest railroad siding to our township. I moved some of my rock hoisting equipment to the rail siding along with a muleskinner and mules to operate it. This would speed up the unloading of wagon boxes.

The railroad set up scales to weigh in our wheat. I drove my Conestoga wagon to the siding and hired a clerk, Henry Bontrager, to keep detailed records on every farmer and every load of wheat we took in. I hired a group of young men from Lindsborg, Kansas to load the wheat into the railroad cars. We contracted with a custom thresher to set up one mile north of my homestead to average the haul distance. We made an agreement with men who hired out as gleaners.

Every buckboard, grain wagon, rock wagon, hayrack wagon or freight wagon was made ready. Every buggy was prepared to haul drinking water and meals to the men along with grain and water for the horses. The older women would keep the food and water coming. During harvest, men and draft animals had five meals each day. Breakfast and supper at home with three meals in the field: a morning break, lunch and an afternoon break. Everyone had a part to play.

The wheat grew tall, filled, ripened, dried and turned to the color of gold waving in the breeze. The harvest began before dawn with a hearty breakfast for man and beast. Dawn broke with every family, draft animal and wagon headed for the fields. The gleaners, able bodied men with sickles, lined up across the field and began the slow eurhythmic process. With one swing the wheat stems were cut, caught in the cradle and released in a windrow behind them. They worked in sync with steady progress through the field. Young boys with hand sickles gleaned the wheat missed so the men could maintain their progress. Women and children raked the wheat into the windrows ahead of the hayracks coming through the field. The older girls became teamsters.

Men loaded the wagons as high as possible

using pitchforks. Each loaded wagon had a tied down wagon cover on top of the wheat. Each hay wagon in the field was drawn by two teams until the wagon reached the road. Then one older girl, our teamster, with one team pulling the loaded wagon, would start down the road to the threshing machine. The wagons were offloaded into the threshing machine and reloaded with straw for the return trip. Two women were stationed at the threshing machine operation to issue a numbered bill of laden, verify the particulars, and sign for each loaded wagon headed for the railroad.

Those big raw-boned Swedes from Lindsborg were a Godsend. The harvest lasted ten days and two days later the last boxcar was loaded and sealed. They loaded fifteen carloads of wheat. We had ordered twelve boxcars and the railroad made three more available for our larger than expected harvest. We loaded all of our wheat and I accepted wheat on consignment from other local farmers to fill out the last boxcar. The clerk had a large envelope for each farmer. The envelope had the farmer's name on it with a listing of each load showing the bill of laden number, loaded wagon weight and the empty wagon weight along with the calculation of bushels in each load. I made arrangements with two of my loaders to meet us on the return trip from Kansas City.

I took my colt pistols from the Conestoga wagon and packed them in my suitcase. Henry and I brought the envelopes and hopped into the train's caboose for the trip to Kansas City. I went to the exchange and sold every boxcar load at top market prices direct to agents of Chicago and Kansas City flourmills. We took the checks to the bank and deposited the funds into a bank account. We paid the freight bill and the exchange fees by check.

We then set down to compute the distribution of the proceeds. We listed all of the common expenses, the freight bill, exchange fees, gleaners, threshing operator, loaders and the clerk. I added a well-earned bonus to the loaders and the clerk. The gleaners and the thresher were paid by the bushel so they benefited from the huge harvest. We then worked out the final settlement with each farmer showing the bushels and net price after the common expenses. We worked out the sharecropper agreement to reflect the net landlord share. The clerk made an accounting to each farmer on his envelope.

The farmers wanted to be paid in coins so we went to the bank where a cashier counted out each net settlement in gold and silver coins and provided a coin pouch for each one. We tagged and placed the coin pouch in each farmer's envelope and tagged a coin pouch for each gleaner, loader, our thresher and for Henry the clerk. I arranged with the Bank to send cashier's checks to my absentee partners in California. I made an arrangement with my Kansas City bank to periodically send a money order to my parents in Ireland from my bank account. We bought and filled four large carpetbags filled with gold and silver in money pouches and settlement documents and bought tickets to McPherson. We strapped on our pistols and boarded the train to return for a meeting at a favorite picnic spot near the Little Arkansas River.

Our loaders, gleaners and our thresher met us in McPherson and we settled with them. My Swedish boys were not given to demonstration but their joy was unrestrained. We were joined by two of my loaders who acted as guards. I armed them with Winchester repeating rifles and we started the trip to the picnic grounds to settle up with the farmers.

We arrived at the settlement grounds at midmorning. Most of Rockville Township was there and seemed curious about our armed guards. They gathered around the wagon in anticipation. I stood up in the wagon box and told them this harvest should be a source of pride for everyone involved. We had put everything we had in it together. It was accomplished through our unity.

Then we got down to the settlement. We all had faith and trust in each other but the settlement was business and trust must be proven by results based on a clear understanding of the facts. I introduced Henry Bontrager, our clerk. Henry proceeded to explain the lists of bills of laden, common expenses and the process. Several farmers had questions about the bills of laden but the women who prepared them were quick to explain and defend their diligence.

Henry stepped down from the wagon and took a seat behind a table with all the envelopes. He called out the name on the first envelope. A farmer stood up with his family and they made their way to the table. His wife and oldest daughter went through the bills of laden, looked over the schedule of wagons unloaded and nodded their approval. The farmer signed the envelope and looked into his coin pouch and fainted. His family was quick to assist him. They were so caught up in reviving him they did not notice the amount.

The next name was called with the same

process and the farmer shouted with joy and began dancing and celebrating with his family. The third farmer went through the same due process and broke into uncontrollable weeping. His whole family joined him. Not one of us dirt farmers had ever seen or dreamed of this much gold.

The settlements took the rest of the morning to complete. The celebration started and lasted till late into the night. There were prayers, rejoicing, food, music and dancing aplenty. We had never seen this much money in our lives. It represented a brand new start for each of us. We had caught the tide at its crest and rode it high onto the shore. The Turkey Red Winter Wheat had turned to gold. 1876 had been a bad year for General Custer but a banner year for the Homesteaders.

I thanked my Lord in heaven for my good fortune. It promised to be everything and more than Kate and I needed to put our lives together.

The Farmer Takes a Bride

Kate and I were planning our wedding in St. John's Church, Louisville, Kentucky for April 20th, 1877. I arrived in the middle of April to a warm welcome of all my relatives and friends. Everyone knew I had become a landowner in Kansas but nobody suspected the extent of my good fortune. Kate and I wanted a grand wedding with all the bells and whistles. I knew her new life would be a sacrifice compared to her comfortable home in Louisville, but she was ready and willing. Her new house plans had been completed and she looked forward to a new beginning.

Kate and her family made all the arrangements. I just followed behind and paid the bills. The whole community pitched in to support us and filled the Church. The bride was beautiful and the wedding went off without a hitch. St. John's was decorated to the teeth. My beautiful bride walking down the aisle with the pipe organ playing on high and the large choir singing gave me goose bumps. The love of my life, who was never at loss for words, was speechless. She just managed to repeat her vows through her tears.

St Johns Church of Louisville, Kentucky

The reception included about two hundred people. My sisters Julia, Mary and Ellen along with their families were present and we talked about our parents so far away. I felt proud of my sisters. They had all established themselves with good husbands and fine families. The struggle in Ireland had not improved. I read every letter my sisters had received from home. I wrote a long letter to my parents. I could not bring myself to explain how well my life was going when I knew the conditions they were living under. I did make it clear we dearly loved America and what this county stood for. I explained that I would soon be a naturalized U.S. Citizen and was proud of it. The wedding had brought my sisters and I together for this wonderful event.

We lingered several days after the wedding. Kate had to get her things together for transport to our new home and I had extra time to spend with my sisters. On April 25th, 1877 we boarded the train for Kansas and a new life together. I hoped Kate would take to my friends, the Buffalo Soldiers, the Kansa Indians, the settlers, my business associates and Nathan Bean.

Laurence(Larry) and Catherine(Kate) Burke

The New House on the Prairie

We arrived at our home, the soddie, about mid-afternoon on a sunny day. Kate had listened to everything I told her but she gasped at the sight. A lonely prairie with a dirt shelter on it. Thank the Lord she soon adjusted and had the vision to see what we had planned to do in the future. She soon was comfortable with all of my friends who came to enjoy her sharp wit and her constant conversation. She left them no choice but to accept her. I think she was happy to find other human beings living in this prairie wilderness.

We received word in December that my mother,

Anne Ryan Burke died December 3rd, 1877. She died without any of her children around her. Dad and Tom were continuing to work the farm but it would never be the same without her. She had been grateful for the support I sent them. She knew all of her children loved her and were succeeding in America. Mom was born in Ireland in 1817 and died at sixty years of age. She was buried in the Loughmore Old Grave Yard without a priest or a marker under the English Penal Code. My pain was beyond words. The Lord willing, someday I will see to her marker.

Kate was home alone the day the Pawnee Indian hunting party showed up. Kate with her quick wit immediately began putting food out on the table. The Indians ate their fill and took with them food they could not eat. The kitchen, the pantry and root cellar were about empty but they did not touch Kate. She was shaken but unbowed. My pioneer wife had proved herself equal to the task.

The Pawnee Indians would not steal anything that slowed them down on the trail and they knew the Buffalo Soldiers were nearby. I reported this to Sergeant Johnson and the Buffalo Soldiers pursued them out of the county. We assumed this would be the end of Kate's adventure with the Pawnees.

The barbed wire fences would stop the Buffalo, the hunting parties and the cattle drives through this area; plus the railheads were steadily moving west.

The homesteaders were feeling better after their success in 1876. 1877 and 1878 had been good but nothing would ever beat the harvest of 1876. The Trading Post was doing well and Nathan Bean and I could not produce limestone fence posts fast enough. Barbed wire was cheap and the Settlers had cash to spend. Homestead improvements were booming.

We ordered lumber for the new house and I cut and carved stone footings and foundations with all the artistry I could come up with. We would start the new livestock barn before the house was finished. This was a busy year and Kate informed me she needed the new house for our baby that was due in January the next year. Kate had done it to me again. I could not deny or explain the joy I felt. The baby would get there first but the new house would be next. We decided to build the new house over the dugout. This would give us a readymade storm and root cellar.

Our baby arrived January 8th, 1879. We called him William Henry Burke. William for his namesake: the founder of Clanwilliamburke in Ireland and my father Henry.

On April 7, 1879 I was granted citizenship in Rice County, Kansas, United States of America. The three of us were finally U. S. citizens. This was a day I would always remember.

The citizens of Little River, Kansas were in the process of Incorporating along with the railroad coming in 1780. This would shorten our haul distance and maybe be a good place to build a church. The Priest was visiting our homesteads on a rotating basis for Services one Sunday each month. This worked well for our community but was difficult in some of the homes and we longed for regular Sunday Mass.

We needed to get busy on our road system all

the way into Little River, which was six miles straight north of our homestead. The homesteaders of our township met and worked out a plan to improve the roads from several miles south of my place to Little River. I had a road grader and stone for the bridges. The settlers would furnish the teamsters and teams along with the labor and we would barter on the rest. With no one objecting, it was agreed.

The lumber for the new house would arrive on the railroad siding in Little River, Kansas. The rock footings and foundations were in and waiting. The house would look like Kate's family home except our conveniences would be a pitcher for water and a path to the outhouse.

Jon de Baca and his merchant wagon train stopped to say goodbye. He said the railroad would make it to Santa Fe sometime next year and this would be his last run. He delivered a large Jack and a Jenny mule, along with four large matched draft mares I had ordered from him. Missouri's finest. I would miss his friendship and the many barters we made together.

I met with Nathan Bean to review our outlook and we agreed the end had come for the Santa Fe Trail. The traffic was down to a few settlers and they were taking to the state roads. I planned to keep the stone quarry going for some time but the railroads were bringing in tree fence posts for cheaper than I could afford to cut limestone posts.

There were still some orders for bridge construction and I had a few special orders to fill. I also had a barn to build with rock foundations and flooring. Nathan said he was in the process of selling most of the stones in the Stone Corral to the railroad to build a roundhouse in Nickerson, Kansas and there was talk of building a stone schoolhouse about one mile south. I agreed to help with the hauling. He would continue selling rock from the Stone Corral and working several farms he had acquired. Nathan and I sold most of the merchandise to a mercantile store in McPherson and settled the open book account between us.

Sergeant Johnson of the Buffalo Soldiers had received orders to close Camp Grierson and to excavate and convey his fourteen dead comrades to Fort Leavenworth. They were to be re-interred with military honors. The Indian and the outlaw threats were over and with the Santa Fe Trail no longer in use they had completed their mission. The Buffalo Soldiers were honorable and brave men who served us well. This detachment had come out of slavery and joined the Union Army and served in the Indian war. Six of them were killed in battle. My Indian friend Red Star, the Kansa Chief, took his people to join his tribe on the reservation. They had been fenced out of their hunting grounds.

This chapter of my life was closing but I would never forget my friends and the way they came to my aid when I had nothing. With them everything was possible. The future is in the land.

After completing the Stone Corral Schoolhouse, we hired a teacher. We found a qualified teacher to work for a small wage, room and board on a local farm. The first day of classes was a community affair. Our first class was all first graders from six to thirty-six years old. We started with several men and women helping out. We organized groups by age and we were off and running. The older and brighter students helped with the younger children as they came along with their studies. We always had an adult there to assist with keeping order.

Once our students got into the routine it worked very well. The students not only had individual help but they heard all the other classes going on. The cross training seemed to assist them in the process. By the time the school year ended we had four grades going on in one schoolhouse. The kids took pride in what they had learned. We used classic books for reading and chalk slates for math. We were sure our kids would be the best in Rice County. Life long friendships were formed in the Stone Corral Schoolhouse.

The Burke Dynasty

I cut stone and carved two large limestone gate posts and placed them at the entrance to my homestead. They guarded the front of our land near the byway for all to see. Monuments to America, the pioneer spirit, our hopes and dreams.

The new house was finally complete and Kate was queen of the manor. She ordered a stained glass window to place at the top of the stairs and it graced the house with light, color and good cheer. Our livestock barn was huge and could be seen for miles. The hayloft could store enough hay to serve through the winter and be a great dance hall after harvest. It had enough grain bins to feed the horses and mules that needed oats when they were working. Plenty of space for buggies, harness, tack, and riding and driving horses.

July 12th, 1881 our second son was born, Edward Michael Burke. Edward was our second son but the first born in our new house. He was named after Kate's father, Michael.

My father, Henry Burke of Loughmore, Ireland died November 1st, 1882. It was a long day for me when I received the news. He died with no male heir in Ireland. My uncle Thomas was in ill health and the land was up for grabs. If I returned to Ireland, my future would be spent in jail. My father was buried in the Loughmore Old Cemetery without ceremony or marker. May the Lord bring us together in the hereafter.

On August 13th, 1883, I received the patent, clear title, to my homestead, 160 acres of our corner of the world. Land: a place to take root and raise a family. Love and land were mine.

Most of the homestead claims in Rice County were filed in the 1870s with a five-year period of qualifying improvements to be made to the property. Congress had relaxed the Tree Claim, tree planting requirements due to the drought in Kansas. Some of the people who filed claims did it for speculation; others got discouraged and quit their claims. But many were honest families trying to make a new start and provide for their families.

I settled with my absentee homesteaders who had left for California in 1874 after the grasshopper plague. They liked the money sent to them as the landlord's share of the sharecropping agreement, but none of them wanted to return. It was up to me to make good on the purchase options. They improved their claims enough to secure the land patents and I honored every option I had. I felt the loss of my friends and neighbors. We needed settlers more than land.

Along with my sharecropping agreements with homesteaders who stayed on the land, I had enough production rights to afford the finest new horse-drawn farm equipment on the market. The settlers cooperated to get crops planted and harvested. Harvest time on the Kansas plains was a time for fellowship and cooperation; it was a sight to behold!

Born on February 27, 1884, Laurence Joseph Burke brightened our lives. The name Laurence was from my French-Norman heritage. William of Clanwilliamburke of Ireland was of French-Norman heritage.

Late in 1884, our church group assembled and made plans to build a church in Little River, Kansas. We named it the Holy Trinity Church of Little River, Kansas. Most of the community worked with us to get the construction completed by May 26th, 1885. Patrick Donnelly and I were sponsors.

Catholic Church, Little River Wi

Patrick Donnelly and I became good friends. His Irish parents had come to Pennsylvania from Ireland and we had much in common. Pat had moved to Kansas just ahead of real trouble in the Steel Mills of Pennsylvania. His cousins were members of the Workingman's Benevolent Association nicknamed the Molly McGuires and were demanding "No more child labor or seventy-hour work weeks or payment in chits or trust conspiracies between National Corporations to victimize the labor force."

The Armed Pinkerton Detectives were bought in to break the strikers and they killed many of the unarmed strikers. The men retaliated. The men were tried and ten of them hanged. Dennis Donnelly, Pat's cousin, was one of the men hanged. Seventy-hour work weeks and child labor continued.

George James Burke, our fourth son, was born July 17th, 1887. Mary Francis Burke, a daughter, was born October 5th, 1889. We could not hide our joy at finally having a daughter.

I was elected to a three-year term as County Commissioner in Rice County, Kansas on November 7th, 1890. My platform was my interest in good roads and schools. I had a record in Rockville Township that supported me and I won with a fair margin. I was a registered Lincoln Republican and loyal to what he stood for.

I ran for reelection in 1893 but was defeated. The economy was down and several other parties ran candidates in the race. I could not overcome the three-way split in the election. Free State Kansans were Lincoln Republicans and thought of themselves as independent Free Traders and not beholden to interference from the government.

Thomas Joseph Burke, our fifth son, was born February 23rd, 1892. We named Thomas after my beloved Uncle Thomas Burke who replaced me on the family farm in Ireland.

Wall Street Moguls made a deal with the railroads to order all available boxcars used for transporting wheat. Their traders stationed the boxcars at the grain stations. They set their purchase price on wheat far below the usual market price. The farmers had no other place to sell their wheat, so with bills to pay and families to feed they were forced to sell.

The traders then parked the loaded boxcars on Kansas City and Chicago railroad sidings and waited for the mills to bid up the price to far above usual market price. The Capital Investors made a fortune but forced the farmers into the same poverty that labor had been forced into. The government was our only hope to resolve the issue. Free trade could not work in a climate of market control and restraint of trade.

I announced my support in 1896 for William Jennings Bryan, a Democratic candidate for President of the United States. The economy was down with every sign of getting worse.

The Wall Street Moguls were pushing congress with Republican support to tighten the amount of silver in circulation and the effect on farm income was devastating. Wall Street Moguls had financed the progress of America and seemed determined to claim every dollar in the economy.

Something had to be done and I believed Bryan could make the system work. The republicans were supporting the idea that when the capital wealth was invested in more jobs the money would trickle down to the workers and farmers. Living on the trickle meant poverty for workers and farmers. The absolute power of capital was being used to devastate the labor market and the farm economy. There was no free trade or bartering left in the economy.

McKinley was the Republican candidate and insisted on running his campaign from his front porch. The Wall Street Moguls had forced his nomination, financed his election campaign and used their monopoly of the syndicated newspaper industry to elect him. Bryan ran his campaign on the railroad doing a whistle stop tour of America. The press devastated Bryan's campaign and he lost the election. McKinley became President in 1897.

Our son William (Bill) graduated from Little River High School in 1896. He did not take to dirt farming but had a head for business. We sent him to Ellen Reitman's in Louisville, Kentucky to enroll in the "Bryant and Stratton Business School." Bill graduated in 1897 with high marks and enjoyed his stay with the Reitmans.

My family and I were all at home when the census taker came for the 1900 U. S. census report. I was proud to report that my family and I were all citizens of the USA. I was fifty years old and proud to be an American farmer and owner of the Fairview Stock Farm. Kate was forty-five years old and planning an addition to our house to include an inside toilet and bath with an added room. Bill was twenty-one and looking to Little River Kansas for a future in business. Edward was eighteen and about ready to take on a farm of his own, raising mules, cows and hogs. Laurence J. was sixteen and doing well in school. He had the ability to listen, solve problems and was a natural leader. George was twelve and never without words. He won every debate he had in school and the county. His wit transcended every conflict. He was very good with animals and had developed a large chicken operation on the farm. Mary was ten and our pride and joy. Thomas was eight, our youngest and everyone's favorite.

Laurence J. and George were ardent followers of John L. Sullivan, an Irishman who had fought his way to becoming the world champion heavy weight boxer. They were both good boxers. I did not approve of them boxing, especially when they lost, but they accepted every challenger. I could never understand how they could put everything they had into wining a fight in the ring, but win or lose they always left the fight as friends with their opponent.

George would knock a man down in a heartbeat if he witnessed abuse to an animal, lady or child. He would get the man on his feet, brush him off and explain the error of his ways. He never held a grudge. I admired him for the way he focused on the deed and forgave the person. Sometimes these men would actually become his friends.

Most of the Fairview Stock Farm income came from selling livestock. I called my boys out to the feed yards and told them to pick any animal they wanted to own. When the stock was sold in Kansas City, what their animal sold for was theirs to keep. They did a fine job, taking care of all the animals equally well. My sons became my partners.

When the stock was ready, we would drive the herd straight north, up the road to Little River, up the main street to the railroad stockyards. We shipped our cows by train to Kansas City. The boys would ride the caboose and tend the cattle. Everything was up to date in Kansas City. They deposited the proceeds to our bank account and I paid my sons for their stock sold.

The Presidential election of 1900 was a repeat of 1896. I supported William Jennings Bryan. Progressive Republican Theodore Roosevelt had been forced into settling for Vice President on the ticket by the Wall Street Mogul Republicans. McKinley and Bryan were running on the same platforms as before. The economy was worse and tensions were high.

Again, the Wall Street Moguls had rigged the nomination of McKinley over his Republican opponent Theodore Roosevelt. Roosevelt ran on a platform of a "Square Deal" by busting the monopolies and trusts. Roosevelt accepted second place on the ticket to placate his Republican followers. The Wall Street Moguls knew the Vice Presidency was a voiceless and powerless position that would put Roosevelt out of the picture in Washington DC.

Again McKinley narrowly won the election of 1900. What they could not predict was the assassination of McKinley September 6, 1901. Roosevelt came to power with all his vim and vigor. He immediately used his "Bully Pulpit" to begin working on laws to promote a "Square Deal" in America. He started lawsuits under Sherman Anti-Trust law of 1890 to break up the trusts and monopolies.

With the trusts and the monopolies busted, fair free press and free trade were restored. The Wall Street Moguls did not lose their capital but they lost their power to control the press and the economy. The forty-hour work week with no child labor was now Federal law. These were rights Patrick Donnelly's family had died for.

US monitory system adopted the Gold Standard March 14, 1900. A blow to the Farmers. The Golden Rule: the owner of the gold makes the rule.

President Roosevelt appointed a Federal

Arbitrator to resolve labor strike issues October 16, 1902. He worked to undue absolute control of labor by management. He set a precedent for bartering between management and labor that restored balance to the economy.

My son Edward Burke married Edith Pearl Burtt on September 3rd, 1902. I deeded the north half of Section 18 to him. The property was just north of our home place. He named it the OK Stock Farm and raised mules, hogs and cattle.

In 1902, while our home upgrade construction was going on, a reporter from the Lewis Publishing Company for "Portraits of Well Known People" interviewed me. He took a great interest in our house plans and included it in his article. Kate and

I completed the upgrade on our house in 1903. We held an open house for our friends and neighbors. We now had modern conveniences, including water in the kitchen and an inside bathroom fully plumbed. The barn could be seen for miles. It was constructed on a rock foundation and with rock floors.

President Roosevelt was elected November 9, 1904. Roosevelt had caught the imagination of Americans and we would follow him anywhere. He was popular with the voters but unpopular with the Republican Party Hierarchy and the Wall Street Moguls. His "Square Deal" worked. I was pleased to support him.

The American Industrial Revolution brought great progress to the country. America went from being a consumer of foreign goods to being a manufacturer and exporter of goods to the world. The progress came from capital invested in the railroads, oil production and refining, mining of iron, coal and precious metals along with the development of water channels, water and electric power. The progress that brought America to power also brought power to Capital monopolies and trusts that controlled the press, labor and trade. Absolute control of capital resulted in absolute poverty to workers and farmers. It also brought America to the verge of a national labor revolt. Theodore Roosevelt used the power of the Presidency to sue the Wall Street Moguls under the Sherman Anti-Trust Law. The government won the suits and it brought an end to control or restraint of a free press and free trade. Roosevelt used the power of the Presidency to force Compulsory Arbitration between Management and Labor. The Arbitration he introduced brought equal rights for labor into the bargaining process. The "Square Deal" balanced our economic system.

Our son Bill Burke married Jane (Jennie) Bush March 27, 1905 in Little River, Kansas. Bill was making a mark for himself in business in Little River. He purchased the Grain Elevator and grain buying business from Mr. Hoffman in Little River, Kansas.

Our son Laurence J. Burke married Alice Fortier November 27, 1906 in Little River, Kansas. Alice was of French decent. She was never without words and loved music. Thereafter when we had a family get together we had music.

I deeded Laurence the north half of Section 20. Laurence with my cooperation as well as that of his brothers managed all the Burke farming operations. Laurence had a gift of bringing people together to get the job done and leave everyone satisfied.

J. P. Morgan bailed out Wall Street Bankers with the approval of the President and congress on November 4, 1907. Roosevelt and Congress started to take action on a Federal Reserve Law to protect the public from further corruption and mismanagement in the Banking System.

Our daughter Mary Burke married Dr. William J. Reidy June 22nd, 1910 in Little River, Kansas. Dr. Reidy had moved to Little River to start his dental practice. It was easy to see they were the perfect couple. They moved into a house close to his practice. Kate and I had a close relationship to Mary. Being an only daughter she had a special place in our hearts.

Our son George Burke married Mary Lois Donnelly April 26th, 1911 in Little River, Kansas.

Mary was given away by her grandfather Patrick Donnelly and George's younger brother Thomas was the best man. Mary's father Mike Donnelly had opposed the marriage. Late at night George drove his buggy to her bedroom window where, with the help of her sister Agnes, she took her things and left with George. Mary's father Mike had become a bitter anti-Christian and a known abuser of his wife and family. Facing George would not be a consideration for him.

Mary taught school and was admired by everyone in the community. She was a bright and determined individual and a great match for George. I deeded George the southeast quarter of Section 17. He named it the Lone Tree Breeding Farm. He started a chicken farm and raised, trained and sold matched team driving horses. Roosevelt ran for President on Progressive party ticket after losing the Republican nomination to Taft in 1916. With three parties running, Wilson the Democrat won the election.

Our youngest son Thomas Burke married Rita Marie Louis April 18th, 1917 in Little River, Kansas. I deeded the home place and the southeast quarter of Section 18 to him. Kate and I moved to Little River to retire and turn the farming over to the boys.

Laurence J. was doing well in managing the farms we owned, sharecropped or custom farmed. A big job and he handled it well.

In 1918, Bill Burke in association with Edward E. Stephenson built and equipped a modern ice house in Little River, Kansas and the Citizens State Bank in 1919. In 1921, Bill and Mr. H. C. Hodgson built the finest hotel found in any small town in Kansas.

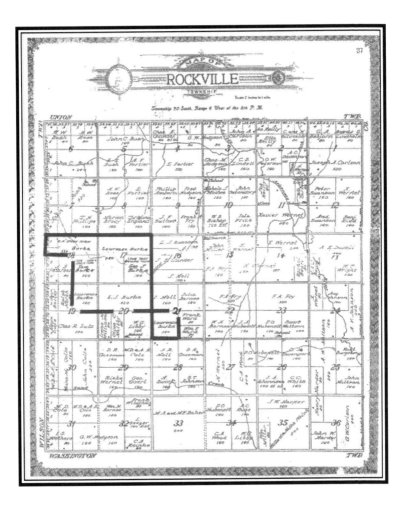

The 1919 Rockville Township map shows the 1,760 acres we owned. In addition, we owned 640 acres in Union Township and 1,120 acres in Odessa Township. The total land we farmed, including sharecrops and custom work, was about 6,000 acres.

The Burke Dynasty

2nd row: George – Laurence J. – William – Thomas – Edward

Front row: Kate – Mary – Laurence Burke

Ireland, Free At Last

Ireland was officially declared a Free State December 2nd, 1922. Finally an end to the bloodletting, Penal Codes and the term "Black Irish" in most of Ireland. The Orangemen of five northern counties refused to be included in the treaty. Free from persecution brought to Ireland by the English Puritan Cromwell in 1641 and the English Protestant King William of Orange in 1690. The Irish Catholics finally had equal rights and a place in the sun. Free at last!

Kate and I planned a trip to Ireland in 1923 to keep my promise that the Lord willing I would return to mark my family graves. We took the train to New York City and booked second-class passage on a ship headed for Queenstown, Ireland.

After arriving in Ireland, we took the train to Templemore. We were the only passengers departing there. The station director hailed a one-horse cart to deliver us to the local hotel. There were no automobiles in Templemore, just a few one-horse carts. We noticed the absence of young people or young families. Most of the people were older spinsters and bachelors. Very few smiles from people we met. Freedom seemed like another word for nothing to do. We stopped to talk to one little old lady and asked about her family. She said, "All my roots are in my garden and I have nothing more to say." The Irish have been through hell and it seemed it would take years to recover.

The next morning, we hired a cart to take us to Loughmore. We drove by my home place and talked to the resident. His name was Richard Burke, a very distant cousin of mine. The home place had changed very little.

We then went to see the Priest as St. Mary's Church. He had little information on the Loughmore Old Grave Yard. We tried to get some information on the location of my mom, dad and Uncle Thomas's graves. He said there was no way to be certain because of the lack of markers. He sensed I was upset over not finding their graves. I caught my breath when he asked if it really mattered. We were Christians and we knew their spirits were not here. I knew he was right. My family were good and decent people with reverence for the Lord that transcended law or dogma. In my deepest heart I knew they had gone to a better life in the hereafter. Whether my family was near or far, I knew the love I felt for them was returned.

The gravestone I ordered was not for them, but for me and my descendants. I wanted my descendants to know my family lived; they mattered and are part of who we are. I ordered a flat stone that called the roll of my dearly beloved including my infant sisters, Anna and Bridget. The large flat stone would be placed upright near the entrance of the graveyard.

IN MEMORY OF

HENRY BURKE – LOUGHMORE

WHO DIED 1ST NOV 1882

AGED 71 YEARS

ALSO

HIS WIFE ANN BURKE

DIED 3RD DEC 1877

AGED 60 YEARS

HIS BROTHER THOMAS BURKE

HIS TWO CHILDREN WHO DIED YOUNG

I had forgotten what real poverty was like. My heart broke for my native land. I would never forget my native land, but my home was in America. We planned to head home the next day. There is no future in the past.

Lord, America Tis of Thee

We boarded the ship in Queenstown for our return trip, saddened by the plight of Ireland but happy to be on the way home. We enjoyed the cruise and arrived in New York Harbor mid-morning. As we came into the Harbor, the Statue of Liberty stood before us with the sun brightening her face. She seemed to be welcoming us home. Kate and I embraced and wept. The Lord had truly blessed us!

Give me your tired, your poor,
your huddled masses yearning to breathe free.
I lift my lamp beside the golden door!

Emma Lazarus

Made in the USA
Charleston, SC
04 September 2014